I, *Geronimo Stilton*, have a lot of mouse friends, but none as **spooky** as my friend CREEPELLA VON CACKLEFUR! She is an enchanting and MYSTERIOUS mouse with a pet bat named **Bitewing**. Creepella lives in a CEMETERY, sleeps in a marble **sarcophagus**, and drives a **hearse**. By night she is a special effects and set designer for SCARY FILMS, and by day she's studying to become a journalist! Her father, Boris von Cacklefur, runs the funeral home Fabumouse Funerals, and the von Cacklefur family owns the CREEPY Cacklefur Castle, which sits on top of a skull-shaped mountain in MYSTERIOUS VALLEY.

YIKES! I'm a real 'fraidy mouse, but even I think Creepella and her family are AWFULLY fascinating. I can't wait for you to read this **fa-mouse-ly funny** and SPECTACULARLY SPOOKY tale!

Geronimo Stilton

Creepella von
Cacklefur

Bitewing

Billy
Squeakspeare

Grandpa
Frankenstein

*A journalist who lives in
Mysterious Valley and
solves spooky cases with
her inseparable pet
bat, Bitewing.*

*A famous writer
and friend of
Creepella.*

*An extremely mad
scientist and an
expert in Egyptian
mummies.*

Snip and Snap

Shivereen

Grandma Crypt

*Troublemaking twins
and expert spies.*

Dolores

Kafka

*Creepella's
favorite niece.*

*She loves spiders, and her
pet is a gigantic tarantula
named Dolores.*

*The von Cacklefur
family's pet
cockroach.*

Booey the Poltergeist

The mischievous ghost who haunts Cacklefur Castle.

Boneham

The butler to the von Cacklefur family, and a snob right down to the tips of his whiskers.

Baby

He was adopted and raised with love by the von Cacklefurs.

Madame LaTomb

The family housekeeper. A ferocious were-canary nests in her hair.

Chef Stewrat

The cook at Cacklefur Castle. He dreams of creating the ultimate stew.

Boris von Cacklefur

Creepella's father, and the funeral director at Fabumouse Funerals.

Chompers

The von Cacklefur family's meat-eating guard plant.

Geronimo Stilton

CREEPELLA VON CACKLEFUR

RIDE FOR YOUR LIFE!

The Swinging Shipwreck

Scholastic Inc.

ISBN 978-0-545-64659-8

Copyright © 2011 Edizioni Piemme S.p.A., Corso Como 15, 20154 Milan, Italy.

International Rights © Atlantyca S.p.A.

English translation © 2014 by Atlantyca S.p.A.

Based on an original idea by Elisabetta Dami.
www.geronimostilton.com

Published by Scholastic Inc., 557 Broadway, New York, NY 10012.
SCHOLASTIC and associated logos are trademarks and/or registered trademarks of Scholastic Inc.

Stilton is the name of a famous English cheese. It is a registered trademark of the Stilton Cheese Makers' Association. For more information, go to www.stiltoncheese.com.

Text by Geronimo Stilton
Original title *Brividi sull'ottovolante*
Cover by Giuseppe Ferrario (pencils and inks) and
Giulia Zaffaroni (color)
Illustrations by Danilo Barozzi (pencils and inks) and
Giulia Zaffaroni (color)
Graphics by Yuko Egusa

Special thanks to Beth Dunfey
Translated by Andrea Schaffer
Interior design by Becky James

12 11 10 9 8 7 6 5 4 3 2 1   14 15 16 17 18 19/0

Printed in the U.S.A.   40

First printing, August 2014

FEAR OF THE BARBER

It was a beautiful **spring** morning in New Mouse City. The sun felt nice and warm on my fur as I ambled over to the **barber** for a furcut.

Oh, pardon me, I almost forgot to introduce myself! My name is Stilton, *Geronimo Stilton*, and I run *The Rodent's Gazette*, the most famous newspaper on Mouse Island.

Anyway, as I was squeaking, that morning I looked at myself in the mirror and realized my WHISKERS needed a little trim. So I scurried over to see Harry Barberello, my furdresser.

When I arrived, there was only one free

seat in the waiting area. I took it and waited my turn. I sat admiring Harry, who wielded his SCISSORS so masterfully, he reminded me of a conductor with his baton.

Every time he finished a new cut, he checked it with a critical eye and exclaimed:

"ABSOLUTELY FABUMOUSE!"

His skill with his shears reminded me of my last adventure in the **Mysterious Valley**, when I found myself snout-to-snout with —

My thoughts were interrupted by a long, skinny paw creeping out from the magazine rack next to me.

"AAAAAHHHHHHH!"

I shrieked, startled.

Two wings appeared next. That's when I realized it was **Bitewing**, my friend Creepella von Cacklefur's pet bat.

"Bitewing! Do you always have to SCARE the whiskers off me?" I muttered.

He giggled and tossed some rolled-up sheets of paper at my snout.

"**OUCHIE!** Watch where you're throwing things — that hurt!" I whined.

Bitewing just ignored me and fluttered toward the door.

"What is this?" I called after him.

"What kind of question is that? It's Creepella's **newest** novel, of course!" Bitewing called as he took flight.

"PUBLISH IT IMMEDIATELY!"

Harry still had a few clients to see before me. I had plenty of time to read Creepella's new ⟨B⟩⟨O⟩⟨O⟩⟨K⟩.

Publish it!

Ouchie!

When I turned to the first page, I realized it told the tale of the adventure I'd just been remembering. What a **crazy** coincidence!

"Why don't you read it aloud?" Harry asked me. "Then we can give Miss **CREEPELLA** some feedback."

He didn't have to ask me twice. I read the title:

"It's called **'RIDE FOR YOUR LIFE!'**"

"Absolutely fabumouse!" Harry said approvingly.

RIDE
FOR YOUR LIFE!

STORY AND ILLUSTRATIONS BY
CREEPELLA VON CACKLEFUR

No Sleep
for You!

The last **SHADOWS** of the night lingered over Squeakspeare Mansion. Geronimo had arrived in Mysterious Valley a few days before. He was hard at work on an enormouse

ENCYCLOPEDIA that told the history of the mansion's ghosts.

He had promised Creepella he would edit it, and he was a mouse of his word.

He was bent over his desk all night long.

At the first light of dawn, Geronimo was too tired to work any longer. So were the mansion's thirteen ghosts. Squeakspeare Mansion was their home, and it was their tradition to clean it from top to bottom at the stroke of midnight each night.

Geronimo had just curled up in bed and closed his eyes when a little cough made him jump.

"Wh-who . . . who's there?" he cried, turning on the light.

Squeakspeare Mansion's butler ghost, Simon Snootysnout, glided toward him.

"What's up, Simon? Why are you still on

your **PAWS** at this hour?" Geronimo asked.

"My dear Mr. Stilton, I had just **dozed off** when there was a knock at the door," Simon explained.

Geronimo sighed. "Who would **knock** at this ridiculous hour?"

Simon's snout twisted into a grimace. "Three **PESTS** — I mean, three nice mouselets and their very peculiar pet. He left a thousand tiny little **FOOTPRINTS** all over the hall floor."

Geronimo had spent enough time in the Mysterious Valley to know exactly who Simon was squeaking about. "Moldy mozzarella! It's the Rattenbaum triplets and their **millipede**, Ziggy." He ducked his snout under the sheet. "Simon, just tell them I went to take a **BATH** in the Slimy

Swamp . . . or better yet, to climb Scram Peak."

"Er, you mean SCREAM Peak, don't you, sir?" the ghost asked politely.

"It doesn't matter where I went! Tell them whatever you want, as long as it makes them go away!" Geronimo replied.

The butler SHOT through the wall. Geronimo breathed a sigh of relief when he heard the triplets' automobile puffing away.

VRRROOOOOOOM!!

"At last I can get some **shut-eye**!"

He turned off the lights again, but as soon as his snout hit the pillow, someone **drummed** on his forehead.

"Send them away, Simon, tell them I left," he muttered, **rolling** over with a loud snore.

Whoever it was would not be so easily discouraged. The next thing Geronimo knew, his blankets were ripped out of his paws.

"**AAAAAHHHHH!**" he squeaked. "What is it? An **earthquake**? A **CAT ATTACK**? A **FIRE**?"

No. Just Creepella, smiling down at him. Next to her was her favorite niece, Shivereen. Behind them, Bitewing fluttered from one side of the room to the other.

"**Wake up! Wake up! Wake up!**" the bat yelled cheerfully.

"Wake up, lazyfur! It's morning, and it's a deliciously gloomy day with a chance of the loveliest little **thunderstorm**," said Creepella.

Geronimo closed his eyes. "Creepella, please let me **sleep**. I worked all night long. . . ." he moaned.

But she wouldn't listen to reason. "Don't squeak, my little furface! There will be no sleep for you today. Don't you know about the **GRAND FAIR**?"

Geronimo could tell from Creepella's hyper-happy tone that any chance of a snooze was gone for good.

"What fair?" he asked, stumbling to his paws.

"I'll explain everything on the way," Creepella replied. "Come on, shake a tail, don't be a snail!"

EVERYMOUSE IS AT THE GRAND FAIR!

Geronimo scrambled into the **Turborapid 3000**, Creepella's convertible hearse, as she kicked it into gear.

"Where are we **going**?" he yawned.

"To **GLOOMERIA**!" called Shivereen from the backseat. "That's where the Grand Fair is held. You'll see, **everymouse** who's anymouse will be there!"

"Exactly what fair are you squeaking about?" Geronimo moaned.

"My dear little batnip, how can you be so **poorly** informed?" Creepella said. "Journalists like you are supposed to

know everything! We're talking about the **ANNUAL GHASTLY GRAND FAIR**, where the rodents of Gloomeria present the most horrible **HORRORS** each year. There will be fear galore, you'll see!"

"Isn't it wonderful?" said Shivereen happily.

"**Ack!**" Geronimo heaved a big sigh.

"And here we are!" announced Creepella, pulling into an open parking space.

A big **Banner** hung over the entrance to the fair.

WELCOME TO THE
ANNUAL GHASTLY GRAND FAIR
IT'S YOUR WORST NIGHTMARE COME TO LIFE!
(NOT RECOMMENDED FOR THOSE WHO SUFFER FROM PANIC ATTACKS AND OTHER FEAR-RELATED SYMPTOMS)

Geronimo tried to scamper off, but Creepella pulled on his paw. "Why are you RUNNING AWAY, my dearest?"

"Because I s-suffer from fear-related symptoms," stuttered Geronimo.

Creepella just laughed and dragged him along with her.

Gloomeria had been transformed. Around them, mice of all ages were enjoying their favorite thrills. Some were **shrieking** with delicious terror, while others were sighing happily with horror.

Creepella made her way through the crowd. "Come on, let's check out the VON CACKLEFUR BOOTH."

"Your family is here?" Geronimo asked.

"Of course!" Shivereen replied. "Didn't I tell you that everymouse is here? Everymouse who loves a good **SCARE**, that is!"

Boneham the butler greeted them with his usual **snooty** air. "Welcome, ladies!" Then he turned to Geronimo and sniffed. "Oh, you're here, too. . . ."

"Where is everyone?" asked Creepella. Boneham **bowed**. "I am here to accompany you, miss." He took her paw and led her through the crowd.

Soon they reached their first stop.

"Here is Chef Stewrat with his amazing **Stinkerrific Stew**," Boneham announced. "The ingredients include extract of fetid socks, **GREASY** napkins, putrid worm stock, essence of **rancid** trout, and the tears of gigantic leeches."

"My mouth is already **watering** with anticipation!" cheered Creepella.

A few feet away were Snip and Snap with a shelf full of **pranks**.

SNIP AND SNAP
✿ Stick-to-your-snout Caramel
✿ Paw-tripping Super String
✿ Ink-spitting Pens.
Plus any other prank you can
dream up!!!

"Hi, Auntie!" cried Snip. "Do you want to try our whisker-curler?"

"No way," replied Creepella briskly. "That is obviously no whisker-curler!"

"Rotten rats' teeth! You never fall for our tricks," cried Snap.

Next Boneham brought the group to **Melodie Dramamouse's** booth, where Madame LaTomb and Howler, the ferocious werewolf canary who lived in her fur, were treating their audience to a few famouse opera arias.

Madame LaTomb was singing her heart out:

"May the wind be always at your tail!
May you pounce on slugs and slimy snails!"
"Bravo!"

"CREEPY!"

All the spectators were enthusiastic . . .
except Geronimo, that is. The musical tastes
of Mysterious Valley were too strange for
his ears!

Bravo!

AAACHOOOO!

The next booth belonged to Grandma Crypt, and it was one of the most **crowded** at the fair. The reason? Inside was a small **STAGE** where Grandma's pet spider, Dolores, led a crew of arachnids in a dance on stilts made of **BONES**!

The von Cacklefur pet cockroach, Kafka, was onstage, too, shaking his antennae to the beat.

"Grandma, what a fabumousely FRIGHTENING idea!" Shivereen exclaimed.

"Thank you, my dear!" Grandma Crypt replied, beaming. "They've been rehearsing

since the last full moon."

But the fair wasn't over, not by a long shot! Over in **UNDEAD BARD CORNER**, Boris von Cacklefur was about to recite his latest melancholy ode, titled "The Mouse in Agony." Creepella, Shivereen, and Geronimo stopped to listen to him.

"Daddy, your work is the most repulsive of them all," Creepella said approvingly.

The Mouse in Agony
by Boris von Cacklefur

The mouse in agony
Meandered down the lane
Thinking of his lost love
And whimpering with pain.

A fat rat demanded,
"Why do you weep into my lap?
Your dreary moaning
Disturbs my ratnap!"

At these cranky words
The mouse regained his pride.
He stuck his snout into the air
As his tail swung side to side!

The last von Cacklefur booth belonged to Grandpa Frankenstein, who was proudly displaying his collection of wrinkled MUMMIES. Above it hung a sign:

SPECIAL PRIZE! ONE FREE
INVENTION PER VISITOR!

"Ooh, a prize! Which invention are you giving out, Grandpa?" Creepella asked.

"Come closer, my dear!" her grandfather replied.

Creepella leaned forward. Her grandfather opened a little box right in front of her snout.

"Achoo...
Aachooo...
Aaachoooo!"

Creepella sneezed three times in a row. With the first sneeze, a little PURPLE cloud formed in front of her. The second produced a GREEN one, and the third created a RED one.

"It's made from the dust of **firefly fossils**!" her grandfather explained proudly.

"**INCREDIBLE!**" shouted Shivereen, impressed.

But her grandfather just nodded silently. "Shhh!" he whispered. "The enemy has ears everywhere!"

"Which enem —" asked Creepella, **peering** at the next booth. "Oh, I get it. . . . You mean Shamley Rattenbaum!"

ONE SNEEZE TOO MANY

Shamley was in front of his booth, looking around eagerly. In his paw he held a magnifying glass. When he saw Geronimo, he smiled warmly.

"Ah! The famouse journalist from New Mouse City! You are the perfect suitor for my adorable granddaughters! How are you, Mr. Stolten?"

"His name is Stilton, S-T-I-L-T-O-N," Creepella told Shamley sharply. Then she turned to Geronimo and muttered, "And I wouldn't get your tail in a twist over his granddaughters. . . ."

Shamley tugged his whiskers. "What bad luck that I have the booth next to these dreadful VON CACKLEFURS!"

"What are you exhibiting, Mr. Rattenbaum?" Geronimo asked. "Your booth looks EMPTY."

Shamley chuckled. "It's not empty. Let me present to you the most *fabumouse* show at the fair — Shamley's Amazing Acrobatic Fleas!"

Shamley's Amazing Acrobatic Fleas

BIRTHPLACE: Jumper's Pass

SIZE: Half a pin's head

SPECIAL SKILLS: Beastly backflips, serious somersaults, critical cartwheels, toxic tumbles, and belly flops

WEAK POINTS: They are really hard to see!

Geronimo leaned in close. "But I don't see **ANYTHING**. . . ."

"Of course not!" exclaimed Shamley. "The fleas are invisible to the naked eye. You need *this*!"

He pawed Geronimo the magnifying glass, and the writer peered through it.

At that moment, Creepella scampered over with her grandfather's BOX between her paws. "Gerrykins you haven't tried out grandfather's new invention," she exclaimed, thrusting the box under Geronimo's snout.

"Creepella, you know I'm **aLLeRgic** to everything!" he protested.

But it was too late.

"ACHOO! ACHOO! ACHOO! ACHOO!"

Four small clouds appeared — first a pink one, then a blue one, then a green one, and then an orange one.

"AAAAAAACHOOOOOOOOOOOOO!"

Geronimo's last sneeze, which formed a big RED CLOUD, was so powerful it sent him flying. He landed SMACK in the middle of Shamley's booth, scattering fleas everywhere.

"Hee, hee, hee!" Bitewing giggled.

"NO! My FLEAS!" shrieked Shamley. "They could be anywhere! Quickly, we must use the magnifying glass to find them."

Geronimo looked guiltier than a gopher in a gerbil burrow. He'd landed on the

magnifying glass, and it had **shattered**.

"You did this on purpose!" Shamley shrieked at Creepella. "You are just as sly and *sneaky* as the rest of your family!"

Grandpa Frankenstein hurried to Creepella's **DEFENSE**. "How dare you squeak to my granddaughter that way, Shamley!"

"She **destroyed** my genius idea!" Shamley protested.

"Hmph! Your genius idea was nothing but a **Silly Sideshow**!" retorted Grandpa Frankenstein.

Achoo!

SHAMLEY'S FLEAS

Oww!

"Why, you blubbering buffoon, I'll . . . I'll MUMMIFY you!" Shamley shouted.

"Just try!" Grandpa Frankenstein cried. "You don't have the guts or the know-how!"

Creepella put her paws between the two rodents to SEPARATE them. Then she led her grandfather back to his booth.

"Calm down, Grandpa," Creepella said. "It's not Shamley's fault. We ruined his sideshow."

But Grandpa Frankenstein was MADDER than a black cat on a mouse-free diet. "Just let me at him! I'll fling him into a pool of piranhas!"

Geronimo tried in vain to soothe Shamley. "You'll find the fleas — I'll help you! Don't worry."

But Shamley just stormed away. "I'm leaving! There will never be peace between

the von Cacklefurs and the Rattenbaums.
Never!"

"What do you think he meant by that?"
asked Geronimo after Shamley had
disappeared into the crowd.

"Oh, it's an ancient legend, longer than an
alligator's tail," began Shivereen.

"A tale with three heroes," continued
Creepella. "The first two are Casper,
Grandpa Frankenstein's **great-grandfather**,
and Reginald, Shamley's **great-grandfather**."

"Who's the third?"
asked Geronimo.

"A FAMOUSE WALNUT TREE!"

Creepella replied.

THE LAST WALNUT

CASPER VON CACKLEFUR

Creepella began to tell the tale.

"Reginald Rattenbaum and Casper von Cacklefur lived **next door** to each other, and spent their mouselinghood scampering back and forth to each other's farms.

They were **best friends** for life — close companions on a thousand **amazing** adventures. They grew up paw in paw, **sharing** every slice of cheese,

REGINALD RATTENBAUM

no matter how small.

"When they were barely more than mouselings, the two friends decided to leave for a **LONG JOURNEY** around the world. They explored lands near and far, collecting many unusual treasures along the way."

"What happened to those treasures?" asked Geronimo. Creepella's story had made him more curious than a cat.

"Well, that's the tricky thing. The von Cacklefurs kept them, while the Rattenbaums **SOLD** them, and then squandered their fortune," explained Creepella.

"How does the **WALNUT TREE** come into the story?" asked Geronimo.

"One winter night, as the two were returning from an excursion in the Mountains of the Mangy Yeti, they met an

exhausted hiker on the edge of the trail.

"Reginald and Casper rescued him and gave him a sip of **blackberry juice** from their canteen.

"When he recovered, the **mysterious** wanderer thanked them warmly: 'I am eternally grateful to you! How can I repay you?'

"Casper and Reginald assured him that they didn't want **anything**, but the wanderer insisted on giving them a gift.

"'I want you to have something special,' he said, opening his battered old bag. He pulled out a small **POUCH** and gave it to the two friends.

"'What is it?' asked Reginald.

"'In this pouch there is a special walnut, **THE WALNUT OF FRIENDSHIP**,' replied the wanderer. 'It symbolizes true friendship.'

"After he squeaked these words, the wanderer went on his way. He disappeared into the fog, and the two explorers continued on their journey.

"When they returned home, they planted the nut on the border between their two farms as a symbol of the eternal friendship between the von Cacklefurs and the Rattenbaums.

"But as the years went by and the walnut tree grew, the two friends passed away, and their descendants began to bicker:

"'The tree belongs to the von Cacklefurs!'

"'Never! It's the Rattenbaums'!'

"The two families were so busy ARGUING that they neglected the tree until it dried up, and so did all its fruit.

"Eventually only one walnut remained. The last walnut is still hanging at the center

of the dried-up branches. When it FALLS on one farm or the other, we will finally be able to say to whom the tree belongs, the VON CACKLEFURS or the RATTENBAUMS," Creepella concluded. "Until then, we can't agree."

The last walnut!

MIMI! WHERE ARE YOU?

"Holey cheese, you'll have a front-page story on your paws when that walnut falls!" exclaimed Geronimo.

"We sure will!" Creepella agreed.

By then, their attention was back over at Grandpa Frankenstein's booth. Word had spread across the fair that he had truly **OUTDONE** himself, and every rodent in Gloomeria wanted to see his **MULTICOLORED** sneeze clouds. A large group of mice and other creatures had gathered outside his booth.

As Geronimo, Creepella, and Shivereen

slipped through the crowd, Shivereen suggested they see every one of the fair's **attractions**.

They began with the **SKELETON TOSS**. Creepella hit the bull's-eye three times in a row and won a little **MUMMY DOLL**. At the Fatal Fishing stand, she won a pair of spotted **piranhas**.

"Auntie, those piranhas are truly **ghastly**! They'll definitely fit right in at Cacklefur Castle, in the tank with all the others," Shivereen said brightly.

Their next stops were the Coffin Crash, the Monster Merry-Go-Round, and the **CASTLE OF HORRORS**.

By the time they took a ride on the Swinging Shipwreck, Geronimo was a mess.

Every time the ship swung through the air, his snout turned greener and greener. At last, he fainted.

"Geronimo, you've grown **softer** than the finest moldy Brie!" Creepella scolded him.

"**You old softie!**" sneered Bitewing.

Raise your paws!

Yippeeee!

The Swinging Shipwreck

Geronimo was too dazed to defend himself. "Are we done yet?"

"Nope! We saved the **BEST** for last," Shivereen replied. "Gloomeria's most famous roller coaster, the **Misguided Ride**!"

"Sounds perfectly horrifying. Let's do it!" exclaimed Creepella.

The roller coaster was shaped like an enormouse **skull**. Instead of cars, it had **COFFINS** full of rodents rolling along the tracks, which disappeared into a tunnel with a terrifyingly high **triple loop** above it.

Geronimo's snout went from **ghost white** to **SLIME GREEN** as he watched the coffins speed up and down. "So, uh, you really want to try it out?" he asked nervously.

Mimi!

"Of course we do!" cried Creepella and Shivereen. They joined the *line* outside the gate. But they were soon distracted by a ratlet whose whiskers were soaked in *tears*.

"Mimi! Where are you?" he cried.

"Poor little mouse," said Shivereen. "Maybe he lost his **pet**."

"Wonder if it's a tarantula, a hornet, or a spitting viper?" mused Bitewing.

Creepella scurried over to the rodent. **"WHAT HAPPENED, MY LITTLE ZOMBIE-WOMBIE?"**

The ratlet burst into tears. "I lost my *sweetheart*. She disappeared inside the roller coaster!"

He threw his paws around Creepella's

neck and **sobbed** into her shoulder. "Mimi and I were *having so much fun* . . . but when our coffin zoomed into the skull's left eye, a gust of icy wind blasted us. Sniff!"

"Strange," commented Creepella. "Then what?"

"I was so scared, I closed my eyes. When I opened them again, my Mimi was gone!"

The ratlet showed Creepella a fur clip in the shape of a **BAT**. "This was all

she left behind. It was lying on the empty seat," he explained. "My Mimi had **very long** fur. It's beautiful, like live snakes. She would never leave behind her favorite clip! Mimi! Where are you?"

"**We have to do something!**" Geronimo declared.

Creepella nodded thoughtfully. "This whole story absolutely reeks of mystery!"

This reeks of mystery!

We have to do something!

It's Our Turn!

Creepella strode to the roller coaster's entrance, where she **RAN INTO** the Rattenbaum triplets. Behind them was their millipede, Ziggy. As soon as he saw Shivereen, he clapped his feet with glee.

The young mouselet tossed a few mummy mold **candies** at him. Ziggy swallowed them in one bite.

"ZIGSLURP!"

The triplets, on the other paw, were less enthusiastic about seeing their longtime enemy.

ZIGSLURP!

"Ugh! It's that **DREADFUL** Creepella!" groaned Tilly.

"Grandfather told us —" Lilly began.

"— that you **ruined** his exhibit!" finished Milly.

"It was an **accident**!" Creepella protested.

"It's true," confirmed Geronimo. "I stumbled and fell on your grandfather's flea theater, but I didn't do it on purpose. You see, I am an extremely CLUMSY rodent. I apologized profusely."

"But . . . aren't you the one —" said Lilly, dumbfounded.

"— who went to climb —" continued Milly.

"— Scream Peak?" asked Tilly.

Geronimo **blushed** from the tip of his

tail to the tips of his whiskers.

Creepella cut them short. "I absolutely must ride this roller coaster to figure out what happened to Mimi. **Let me pass!**"

The triplets blocked the entrance.

"Don't even think about it!"

"How dare you cut in front of us!"

"It's our turn!"

An EMPTY coffin pulled up in front of them. The Rattenbaums scurried onboard with a triumphant YELP. Ziggy tried to drag his feet, but the triplets yanked him in. They buckled their seat belts, and the coffin shot off like a **rocket**, zipping toward the big skull.

First the coffin zoomed HIGH UP into the skull. It disappeared into the right eye, then came DOWN through the nose.

Creepella kept her eyes locked on her three archenemies as they screamed with delight.

In the coffin's backseat, Ziggy had many of his little feet over his eyes. "**My poor little bug bite!**" said Shivereen, shaking her snout.

The last part of the ride was invisible from the ground. The little coffin entered

the left eye, did three very fast loops, and began the *long descent* toward the exit.

Creepella waited patiently for the coffin to reemerge from the TUNNEL.

"Ghastly gravestones!" she exclaimed as soon as it appeared. "It's just as I feared. . . ."

Inside the coffin was only poor Ziggy the millipede, his trembling feet still over his eyes.

Lilly, Milly, and Tilly had disappeared!

TWISTS AND TURNS

Creepella helped Ziggy scramble out of the coffin. The little millipede had a bad case of the **shakes**, and Shivereen stroked his head to calm him.

Creepella wanted to know more, so she talked to Ziggy in Millipedese.

"ZIGZIG ZiGi ZiGi?"

Ziggy replied, **"ZiGGi Z-ZiGGi!"**

"ZiG ZiGGu," concluded Creepella.

Geronimo looked at them *impatiently*.

"So, what did he say?"

"It's past time you learned to squeak **Millipedese**!" Creepella scolded him. "Ziggy said that he didn't see **anything** because his eyes were shut tight. But when they entered the skull's left eye, he felt a freezing gust, like the breath of a phantom."

"A **phantom**?" whispered Geronimo. "Are you saying there's a phantom inside the eye of the roller coaster?"

"I don't know," replied Creepella. "But I intend to **FIND OUT**!"

Creepella leaped into the coffin, and Shivereen jumped in beside her.

"No! Creepella, you and Shivereen can't go in there alone, it's far too **DANGEROUS**!" Geronimo cried.

He **PULLED** her by the paw, trying to make her climb out.

"You're right, you rotten little pumpkin," Creepella agreed. "We shouldn't go in there alone." **Faster** than the smell of rancid stew travels, she pulled out a short ROPE and tied his paw to her own.

"Creepella? **What are you doing?**" sputtered Geronimo.

"We'll be **safe** as long as you're with us!"

Now let's go!

Creepella said sweetly. "Now **LET'S GO**!"

The coffin was just starting to move when Shamley made his way through the crowd, **SHRIEKING** like a vampire who's just met his first garlic clove.

"You!" he squeaked at Creepella. "Tell me what happened to my adorable granddaughters!"

Creepella looked up at him **calmly**. "I don't know, but I'm about to find out!"

At that moment, the coffin **ZOOMED AWAY** like a hyperactive hamster on a treadmill. Shivereen clapped her paws in excitement.

"How deliciously terrifying!"

she cried as the coffin zigzagged down the tracks at a supersonic **SPEED**.

"Wow! This is better than a trip to the **CEMETERY**!" squealed Creepella. "Don't you just love it?"

Geronimo didn't respond. He had *fainted* again.

Shivereen quickly brought him around with some smelling salts from her purse. "Look, Auntie," she said. "Geronimo changed colors again. First he was *green*, now he's **YELLOW**!"

"Just like Chef Stewrat's famous Moldy Cheddar Surprise!" laughed Creepella.

But a moment later, she was serious again. "We must pay attention! In a couple seconds, we'll **enter** the skull's left eye."

As the coffin whizzed into the dark tunnel, Geronimo exclaimed, "It's so **DARK** in here, I can hardly see my whiskers in front of my snout!"

Suddenly, Shivereen and Creepella felt an **icy gust** pulling on their fur. A moment later, they'd been **SUCKED** into an enormouse vortex!

And because Creepella and Geronimo were attached at the wrist, he was **PULLED** into the darkness along with her!

TRAPPED!

Creepella, Geronimo, and Shivereen were suspended in midair for a moment. Then they fell into something soft.

"But where are we?" asked Shivereen, trying to scramble up but slipping back down.

"I don't know. It seems to be . . . a net. Like the kind trapeze mice use," exclaimed Creepella, peering into the darkness around them.

"How is Geronimo?" asked Shivereen. She began to BOUNCE up and down in the net.

"He fainted . . . again. But I know just how to wake him up!"

Creepella leaned over her unconscious friend and untied the little rope from their paws. Then she stuck Grandpa Frankenstein's BOX under his snout.

A moment later, Geronimo woke up with a series of sneezes. Little colored clouds lit up the space around them.

BOING!
BOING!
BOING!

Achoo!

 TRAPPED!

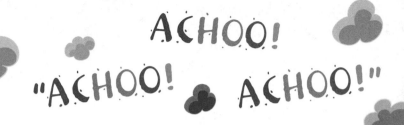

ACHOO!
"ACHOO! ACHOO!"

In the light of the clouds, Creepella and Shivereen could see where they'd landed. There was a net strung in the center of the structure supporting the roller coaster's **GIGANTIC** skull.

After Geronimo's fifth and final sneeze, **darkness** fell once more. It was so still, the only sound was Geronimo's teeth **chattering** in fear.

"H-how do we get down from here?" he stammered.

Before Creepella could respond, they heard a loud **CLICK**, and the net closed around them!

"Tattered tarantulas, now we're really TRAPPED!" exclaimed Shivereen. She sounded rather excited about it.

"Shh!" said Creepella. They fell silent, and then they all heard it: a soft, rhythmic flutter. The noise seemed to be getting closer and closer, until it was right next to the net.

"Wh-who's there?" squeaked Geronimo.

FLAP! FLAP! FLAP!

"Oh, I'd recognize the beat of those wings anywhere. It's **Bitewing**!" said Creepella.

"Hi, Creepella! Hi, Shivereen!" their pet bat greeted them.

"Bitewing, how did you find us?" asked Shivereen.

Bitewing fluttered around the net.

"I didn't see you come out of the skull, so I came to **FIND** you. I flew into the left eye, and then I heard your squeaking and saw the br**i**ght clouds. . . ."

"What a good little batty-watty you are!" cooed Creepella.

But Bitewing wasn't finished yet. "I have a **SURPRISE** for you."

Creepella reached through the net's webbing, and Bitewing dropped something into her paw.

"Aha! It's Gasher, the **scorpion** who can cut through anything!" she exclaimed. "He's one of Grandpa Frankenstein's pesky little monsters. Gasher can slice through any CORD," she explained to Geronimo.

The little monster quickly snipped through the links of the net. A minute later, Creepella, Shivereen, and Geronimo landed on the ground with a thud. Creepella stored Gasher in her pocket.

While Creepella was brushing off her dress, Bitewing screeched, "Don't you have something for me, Creepella?"

"Of course I do, my darling! I always have some of your favorite spicy worm candies with me," said Creepella, TOSSING them into the air. "Here's a reward for a job well done."

Bitewing caught them in midair.

"Yum! My favorite!"

THE SEARCH FOR CLUES

CREEPELLA, Geronimo, Shivereen, and Bitewing inspected every inch of the black tent that covered the skull's base, looking for a way out.

After a few minutes, Shivereen said, "Auntie, look! There's a **RIP** here!"

The little group scurried through the hole till they reached the outside of the tent.

"Finally!" sighed Geronimo. "But . . . where are we?"

"At the back of the Misguided

Ride," replied Creepella. "Let's take a look."

"**OUCHIE!**" Geronimo cried, hopping on one paw. "Something **POKED** me!"

Creepella hurried over to him. Stuck in her friend's paw was a *fur-pin* engraved with a cockroach and the initials **T.R.**

"AHA! I KNEW IT!"

"Wh-what?" asked Geronimo.

"We've found **TRACES** of the triplets!" Creepella said triumphantly.

"What does this have to do with the triplets?" Geronimo asked.

Creepella rolled her eyes. "Geronimo-mo! These **INITIALS** don't tell you anything?"

Geronimo tugged at his whiskers.

"Hmm. 'T.R.' Does it mean Thomas Rattola, the famous **poet**?"

Creepella shook her snout.

"Hmmmm . . . how about Theodora Rattolucci, the great **FiLM** director?

"Try again, you silly scatterbrain!" snickered Bitewing.

"**I'VE GOT IT!**" said Geronimo. "Timothy Ratting, the notorious horror novelist!"

"Geronimo, you're more clueless than a baby kitten! It stands for Tilly Rattenbaum, of course!" Shivereen yelled in exasperation.

"Of course! Why didn't I think of it before?" Geronimo said, smacking his snout. "But what in the name of string cheese is Tilly's fur-pin doing here?"

"The triplets must have passed through here," said Creepella. "We must scour this area for **clues**!"

They turned their snouts to the ground around them. A few feet away, Creepella spotted a shiny object. It was a barrette with the initials L.R. "Lily Rattenbaum! We are on the right track!"

"Look there! Near the **MOUSEHOLE**!" Creepella picked up a ribbon labeled M.R.

"It's MEILO'S. Very good. Let's go down!

"Go down? In what sense?" asked Geronimo, looking worried.

"In the sense of underground," replied Creepella decisively. "We all have to go down this mousehole!"

A Trim?

On the mousehole were the words **DO NOT OPEN!**

"The triplets must have gone down here. We have to follow them," exclaimed Creepella. "Bitewing, you go FIRST. You can lead us through the dark."

Bitewing zoomed into the hole. "Come on! There's a ladder !"

Creepella and Shivereen descended one after the other. Geronimo glanced at the dark passage and gulped. He was afraid to follow, but on the other paw, he didn't want to be left alone.

Geronimo finally followed them into the mousehole.

The ladder led to a **DAMP** and NARROW corridor. The three rodents groped their way along it, following a faint light in the distance. It was coming from a door that stood ajar. Without any hesitation, Creepella threw it **OPEN WIDE**.

"Where are we?" asked Geronimo.

The walls of the room were covered with **mirrors** of every size and shape. It looked like an abandoned funhouse.

"*Wow! This is fabumouse!*" exclaimed Shivereen, admiring herself in a mirror that warped her reflection.

While she and Geronimo had fun
MAKING FACES at each other,
Creepella inspected their surroundings
more closely.

She picked up a **bottle** of fur
dye and a curler from the ground.
"Hmm . . . interesting."

At that moment Geronimo, who
was hopping up and
down in front of a
mirror, lost his balance
and bumped into the wall.
"**YEE-OUCH!**" he
exclaimed.

The mirror covering
that part of the wall
turned with a CLICK,
revealing a hidden
door.

"Well done! You did something right for a change!" cheered Creepella, hurrying to open the door.

Behind it, they found a **ROOM** full of boxes, mannequins, armchairs, and newspapers. In the center, on a pile of magazines, stood an enormouse glass JAR.

"Hey, there's something inside it!" Shivereen pointed out.

Lying on a bed of algae inside of the jar was a mysterious crab with big red claws, sleeping soundly.

"But why is there a crab in a jar in this abandoned STOREROOM?" asked Geronimo.

"I was wondering that, too," Creepella replied.

The crab opened an eye and stretched.

Shivereen jumped. "Auntie, check out those claws! They look like SCISSORS!"

The crab's claws were, in fact, as sharp as knife **BLADES**.

"Good observation, Shivereen!" Creepella said. "I **SUSPECT** this crab is not like other crabs."

"What makes it special?" asked Geronimo.

Creepella snorted. "Oh, Gerry Berry, can't you tell? This is one of the world-famouse **BARBER CRABS**!"

"Auntie, look! There's a BUSINESS CARD inside the jar," Shivereen said.

She read aloud:

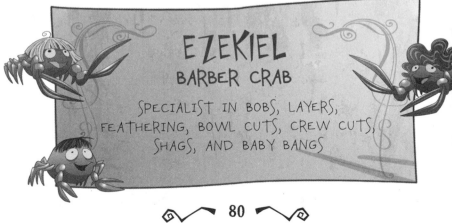

EZEKIEL
BARBER CRAB

SPECIALIST IN BOBS, LAYERS, FEATHERING, BOWL CUTS, CREW CUTS, SHAGS, AND BABY BANGS

Creepella approached the crab tentatively.

"TIRITUTI TAG?"

The crab yawned, and then lazily replied,

"TARITERI TIG?"

"TOG!" concluded Creepella.

"Don't tell me you squeak his language, too?" grumbled Geronimo.

"Geronimo, everyone in the Mysterious Valley speaks **Crabese**. You must learn it too!" Shivereen said scornfully. "Ezekiel said that he was **brought** here in the dead of night, but he doesn't know why."

Creepella smoothed her long fur. "I'm tempted to take advantage and get a little fur **trim**. . . ."

Suddenly, from behind a pile of crates, they heard a shrill squeak:

"Hey, you!"
"We're in here!"
"Help us!"

"The Rattenbaum triplets! We found them!" Geronimo exclaimed.

How cute!

Tarita tig?

Tig tog!

A Phantom Suspect

Creepella cleared a way through between the boxes. Behind them was a row of barber's chairs. The Rattenbaum triplets and another mouselet were seated there, their fur tucked under big **helmets** and their paws tied with ribbons to the pawrests.

"I knew it!" said Creepella triumphantly.

For once, the Rattenbaums seemed happy to see her.

"CREEPELLA!" shrieked Tilly

"You came —" whimpered Milly.

"— to free us!" cried Lilly.

Geronimo, Shivereen, and Bitewing

peeked out from behind the boxes.

"Geronimo! You saved us! Our hero!" the triplets squealed.

Creepella snorted. She swiftly **untied** the knots that bound the mouselets.

"You're Mimi, right?" she asked the fourth mouselet, who had very long, dark fur.

"How did you know?" the mouselet responded in **surprise**.

Geronimo smiled at her. "We met your **sweetheart**. He was crying so hard —"

"— **MUSHROOMS** grew on his eyelids!" Shivereen finished.

"How did you get here?" asked Creepella.

"We were in the eye of the **SKULL** —" Tilly began.

"— when we were sucked from our seats by an **icy draft**!" Milly put in.

"The Fur Phantom caught us in a net —" continued Lilly.

"— and he put them in a **VAN**, just like he did to me!" concluded Mimi. "He sneaked us out of the fair, made us go down into a mousehole, and **IMPRISONED** us here!"

"The **FUR PHANTOM**? What does he look like?" asked Creepella.

"He is very tall and **THIN**, like a headstone in an old cemetery," Mimi answered.

Creepella was perplexed. "I've never known a ghost to drive a van."

"And I still don't understand what the **BARBER CRAB** has to do with it," added Geronimo.

"We'll find out! First we need to free Ezekiel and **GET OUT** of here," declared Creepella.

But when they scurried back through the boxes again, they were in for an ugly surprise.

Ezekiel's jar was EMPTY!

A CREEPY SCENE

"Stop where you are!" an imperious squeak commanded them.

"AAAAAHHHHHHH!"

shrieked Geronimo in terror.

"AAAAAAAAAHHHHHHH!"

the triplets screamed together.

A **ghost** that was tall and thin as a dried-up rind of Parmesan appeared out of nowhere.

He glided toward

them, brandishing the crab threateningly.

"I am the FUR PHANTOM!" he yelled spookily. "And you are my prisoners!"

"Let Ezekiel go, you moldering mummy dropping!" yelled Creepella.

The phantom laughed scornfully. "Never! And if you want me to let you go, you better do what I tell you!"

"Forget it!" snapped Creepella, giving him a withering look. "But just out of curiosity, what exactly do you want us to do?"

The phantom took a step forward, clicking the scissors of his enormouse crab. "You must CUT your fur! All of it — no exceptions," he said darkly.

Creepella and Shivereen erupted into laughter.

"Crumbly corpses! That's the funniest thing I've heard all week," Shivereen hooted.

"What do you want with our **fur**?" Mimi asked.

Instead of responding, the phantom turned to the triplets. **"I'LL START WITH YOU THREE!"**

The Rattenbaums crossed their paws and shrieked in fear.

"Cut our fur?" screamed Lilly.

"Don't even squeak about it!" yelled Milly.

"We'd rather stay trapped down here. . . ." said Lilly.

"For the rest of our lives!" the triplets concluded together.

WHOM THE CRAB CUTS

The phantom was shocked by the triplets' protest. For a moment, he was as motionless as a mummy.

Creepella saw her chance and took it. *Faster* than a cat with a ball of yarn, she snatched the crab out of his paws!

"Off with the sheet!" she cried, using Ezekiel's scissor claws to shred the white fabric covering the phantom. "You mess with the crab, you get the claws!"

With just a few CLEAN cuts, Creepella revealed the phantom's true identity.

"Trembling toadstools!" said Shivereen in shock. "You're —"

"Mopsy Furmouse!" Mimi cried.

In front of them was a rodent with a seemingly endless beehive furdo.

"Who on earth is Mopsy Furmouse?" asked Geronimo.

Off with the sheet!

The triplets looked at him like he'd just come from the time of the cavemice.

"What? Everyone knows who Mopsy is!" protested Lilly.

"She's the most famouse furdresser in Horrorwood!" added Milly.

"She styles all the stars!" explained Tilly.

"I knew it was her," commented Creepella, stroking Ezekiel's shell lovingly. Then she turned and gave Mopsy her most INTIMIDATING glare. "What I don't understand is why she did all this!"

Mopsy was totally cowed. "I am ruined! RUINED!" she sniveled.

Creepella took pity on her. "Why don't you tell us what's going on?"

Mopsy took a deep breath. "Well, I was working . . . SOB . . . on the set of the film *Spooks in the Snowstorm* . . . SNIFF . . .

with Sylvia Cinemouse."

"Yes, I've heard of it," said Creepella. "It stars the famous Robert Rattinson and Kristen Stewrat."

Mopsy stopped crying and grew **ANGRY**. "Don't mention those mangy sewer rats! This is **ALL THEIR FAULT**!"

"What happened?" asked Creepella.

Kristen Stewrat

Robert Rattinson

"I've been working on their furstyles for months, and now all of a sudden they tell me that for the finale, they must wear two very long **wigs** the color of a thundercloud. And they need the wigs by tomorrow!"

"That's why you wanted our **fur**!" exclaimed Shivereen.

Mopsy began to whimper. "I didn't have a choice! The only way to make wigs . . . **SOB** . . . that long and of that color is to use lots of real fur and dye it gray.

"I was just desperate!" she sobbed. "But then I saw . . . **SNIFF** . . . all the mouselets with long fur in line for the roller coaster and . . . **SOB** . . . the idea came to me."

"But how did you capture us?" asked Creepella.

Mopsy blushed redder than pizza sauce. "I used the **GIGANTIC HAIR DRYER** from the set of *Little Barbershop of Horrors*. I reversed it, so that instead

of drying fur, it sucked the mouselets into a net. . . ."

"And you brought us here!" concluded Creepella.

"I'M SORRY! I only wanted your fur. If I don't get wigs for the film as soon as possible . . . SOB . . . my career is over! Done! Finished!"

Shivereen was moved. "Poor mouse! Of course, she made a mistake, but she's sorry. And she's in trouble!"

Geronimo nodded. "Can't we help her?

Creepella smiled. "I think so. I just had a marvemouse idea, but to make it work we must return to the fair!"

HAPPY SNEEZES!

Geronimo couldn't wait to get out of there. "Great! Let's get out of this . . . of this . . . what is this place, exactly?"

"This is the **WAREHOUSE** where I store supplies for my salon," Mopsy replied. "Follow me!"

When they entered the next room, Mopsy explained, "This is my collection of mirrors. To bring the mouselets here without being noticed, I used the secret passage by the mousehole."

She flicked a mirror that hid a door. "But from here you can go directly to the salon."

The little group started up a staircase. Soon they ended up inside Fantastical Fur, the **CHICEST** salon in Gloomeria.

"Mopsy, would you trim our **bangs**?" begged the triplets.

"Not now!" said Creepella. She had other plans. "We need to go back to the fair."

Creepella led them back to Grandma Crypt's booth, where the **spiders** were still dancing wildly. She took her grandmother aside and *whispered* something in her ear.

"But of course, my dear," agreed Grandma Crypt. "We need just a few minutes." She clapped her paws three times, and the spiders stood at attention. Then, as one, they began to **WEAVE** an enormouse web of fabric.

FIF FIF FIF FIF

The fabric **GREW** and **GREW**. Soon it had transformed into a silvery fleece. In a few minutes, two very long, shiny gray wigs were ready.

Mopsy began to hop up and down with happiness. "You saved my tail!" she rejoiced, hugging Creepella.

But Creepella was already on another mission. She took Mimi by the paw and scampered over to the roller coaster.

In front of the line, **DRIPPING** with tears from snout to paw, was Mimi's sweetheart. When he saw her, he almost **fainted** with joy.

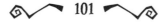

My Mimi!

"Roger! My darling little cheese puff!" said Mimi, running to meet him.

"Our work here is almost done!" cried Creepella, scurrying away again. Shivereen, Geronimo, and the triplets hurried after her.

"But where . . . PANT . . . are we going?" asked Geronimo.

Wait up!

Run, Geronimo!

Hurry up!

Creepella didn't bother replying. She **stopped** only when she'd reached Shamley Rattenbaum's booth.

"Grandfather, we have returned!" cried Milly, hugging him.

"Safe and sound!" said Lilly.

"And it's all because of Creepella!" finished Tilly.

Shamley was **overjoyed** to see his granddaughters, but he couldn't even bring himself to look at Creepella.

She didn't let that stop her. "Mr. Rattenbaum, I'm very sorry to have **RUiNeD** your flea theater. But I have brought you something to make it right."

With that, she placed Ezekiel on the table where the flea theater once stood. "This is Ezekiel. He is a very **SKILLED** barber crab," she explained. "If you ask him *nicely,*

maybe he'll cut fur for free in your booth."

The triplets **smiled** as they watched Creepella slink away.

"Creepella may cause a lot of trouble —"

"— but she is also very —"

"— generous!"

Shamley cut them off. "Enough chatter; let's get to work. With this enormouse **CRUSTACEAN** in our paws, we'll have the most popular booth in all of Gloomeria!"

Creepella returned to **GRANDPA FRANKENSTEIN'S** stand, where everyone was sneezing cheerfully.

The colored clouds were everywhere!

"Achoo!" "Achoo!" "Achoo!" "Achoo!" "Achoo!" "Achoo!"

They lit up the sky like fireworks. For once, it was impossible for **NIGHT** to descend on Gloomeria.

Once Geronimo was finally done **sneezing**, Creepella had a suggestion for him. "Let's go on the Misguided Ride again!"

Geronimo turned paler than mozzarella. "Haven't we had enough **thrills** for one day?"

Creepella just laughed. "Of course not! **IN GLOOMERIA, YOU CAN NEVER GET ENOUGH CHILLS AND THRILLS!**"

NOTHING TO CUT!

When I read the last line of Creepella's novel, my squeak trembled lightly. So many memories! **AND THRILLS GALORE!** In the barbershop, there were a few moments of silence.

Harry Barberello was the first to squeak. First he punched his **SCISSORS** into the air, and then he shook his comb and exclaimed,

"Magnificent! Fabumouse!"

All Harry's clients began to clap their paws and exclaim praises.

"Terrific!"

"You should **publish** it immediately!"

"I want three copies!"

"I'll take **ten**!"

Harry beckoned me to sit down on the chair in front of the **mirror**.

I shook my snout and headed for the exit. My whiskers were still trembling with $fear$ at the memory of that **adventure**. I'd had

enough scissors for one day!

My whiskers could wait another week, but the publication could not! With Creepella's MANUSCRIPT clutched in my paws, I headed straight for the office of *The Rodent's Gazette*.

"Here is Creepella von Cacklefur's new novel! We need to **PRINT** it immediately!"

Done!

My colleagues looked at the manuscript in surprise. "Just like this? You have nothing to add and nothing to cut?"

"Nothing to ADD and nothing — I mean nothing — to CUT!" I replied, chuckling. Don't get me wrong, dear reader, most manuscripts need to be edited. But Creepella von Cacklefur's latest book was perfect just as it was: a fabumouse, bestselling thriller!

Here is a new bestselling thriller!

Fantastic!

If you liked this book, be sure to check out my other adventures!

#1 THE THIRTEEN GHOSTS

#2 MEET ME IN HORRORWOOD

#3 GHOST PIRATE TREASURE

#4 RETURN OF THE VAMPIRE

#5 FRIGHT NIGHT

#6 RIDE FOR YOUR LIFE!

Don't miss any of my other fabumouse adventures!

#1 Lost Treasure of the Emerald Eye

#2 The Curse of the Cheese Pyramid

#3 Cat and Mouse in a Haunted House

#4 I'm Too Fond of My Fur!

#5 Four Mice Deep in the Jungle

#6 Paws Off, Cheddarface!

#7 Red Pizzas for a Blue Count

#8 Attack of the Bandit Cats

#9 A Fabumouse Vacation for Geronimo

#10 All Because of a Cup of Coffee

#11 It's Halloween, You 'Fraidy Mouse!

#12 Merry Christmas, Geronimo!

#13 The Phantom of the Subway

#14 The Temple of the Ruby of Fire

#15 The Mona Mousa Code

#16 A Cheese-Colored Camper

#17 Watch Your Whiskers, Stilton!

#18 Shipwreck on the Pirate Islands

#19 My Name Is Stilton, Geronimo Stilton

#20 Surf's Up, Geronimo!

#21 The Wild, Wild West

#22 The Secret of Cacklefur Castle

A Christmas Tale

#23 Valentine's Day Disaster

#24 Field Trip to Niagara Falls

#25 The Search for Sunken Treasure

#26 The Mummy with No Name

#27 The Christmas Toy Factory

#28 Wedding Crasher

#29 Down and Out Down Under

#30 The Mouse Island Marathon

#31 The Mysterious Cheese Thief

Christmas Catastrophe

#32 Valley of the Giant Skeletons

#33 Geronimo and the Gold Medal Mystery

#34 Geronimo Stilton, Secret Agent

#35 A Very Merry Christmas

#36 Geronimo's Valentine

#37 The Race Across America

#38 A Fabumouse School Adventure

#39 Singing Sensation

#40 The Karate Mouse

#41 Mighty Mount Kilimanjaro

#42 The Peculiar Pumpkin Thief

#43 I'm Not a Supermouse!

#44 The Giant
Diamond Robbery

#45 Save the White
Whale!

#46 The Haunted
Castle

#47 Run for the Hills,
Geronimo!

#48 The Mystery in
Venice

#49 The Way of
the Samurai

#50 This Hotel Is
Haunted!

#51 The Enormouse
Pearl Heist

#52 Mouse in Space!

#53 Rumble in
the Jungle

#54 Get Into Gear,
Stilton!

#55 The Golden
Statue Plot

#56 Flight of the
Red Bandit

The Hunt for the
Golden Book

#57 The Stinky
Cheese Vacation

#58 The Super
Chef Contest

Don't miss my journey through time!

MEET
GERONIMO STILTONIX

He is a spacemouse — the Geronimo Stilton of a parallel universe! He is captain of the spaceship *MouseStar 1*. While flying through the cosmos, he visits distant planets and meets crazy aliens. His adventures are out of this world!

#1 Alien Escape

#2 You're Mine, Captain!

Don't miss these exciting Thea Sisters adventures!

Thea Stilton and the Dragon's Code

Thea Stilton and the Mountain of Fire

Thea Stilton and the Ghost of the Shipwreck

Thea Stilton and the Secret City

Thea Stilton and the Mystery in Paris

Thea Stilton and the Cherry Blossom Adventure

Thea Stilton and the Star Castaways

Thea Stilton: Big Trouble in the Big Apple

Thea Stilton and the Ice Treasure

Thea Stilton and the Secret of the Old Castle

Thea Stilton and the Blue Scarab Hunt

Thea Stilton and the Prince's Emerald

Thea Stilton and the Mystery on the Orient Express

Thea Stilton and the Dancing Shadows

Thea Stilton and the Legend of the Fire Flowers

Thea Stilton and the Spanish Dance Mission

Thea Stilton and the Journey to the Lion's Den

Thea Stilton and the Great Tulip Heist

Thea Stilton and the Chocolate Sabotage

Thea Stilton and the Missing Myth

1. Mountains of the Mangy Yeti
2. Cacklefur Castle
3. Angry Walnut Tree
4. Rattenbaum Mansion
5. Rancidrat River
6. Bridge of Shaky Steps
7. Squeakspeare Mansion
8. Slimy Swamp
9. Ogre Highway
10. Gloomeria
11. Shivery Arts Academy
12. Horrorwood Studios

1. Oozing moat

2. Drawbridge

3. Grand entrance

4. Moldy basement

5. Patio, with a view of the moat

6. Dusty library

7. Room for unwanted guests

8. Mummy room

9. Watchtower

10. Creaking staircase

11. Banquet room

12. Garage (for antique hearses)

13. Bewitched tower

14. Garden of carnivorous plants

15. Stinky kitchen

16. Crocodile pool and piranha tank

17. Creepella's room

18. Tower of musky tarantulas

19. Bitewing's tower (with antique contraptions)

DEAR MOUSE FRIENDS,
GOOD-BYE UNTIL
THE NEXT BOOK!